World of Reading

Pre-1

W9-AOY-470

Disney Junior

MICKEY MOUSE FUNHOUSE

HOMESICK!

Adapted by **Sheila Sweeny Higginson**

Based on the episode by **Sib Ventress**

Illustrated by **Loter, Inc.**

DISNEP PRESS

LOS ANGELES • NEW YORK

SUSTAINABLE FORESTRY INITIATIVE

Certified Chain of Custody
Promoting Sustainable Forestry

www.sfiprogram.org
SFI-01415

The SFI label applies to the text stock

Today is Funny's first picnic!

Goofy has an umbrella.
Watch out, Donald!

Where will the picnic be?
Daisy wants someplace warm.
Donald wants a nice view.
Minnie wants moonlight.

Funny gets to choose a place
for the picnic.

Everyone goes up, up the
Stairs to Anywhere.

"ACHOO!"
Funny sneezes.
Everyone goes flying!

They land in a place that is
very warm.

It is the desert!

The desert is *not* a good
place for a picnic.

"My sandwich!" says Donald.

A desert wind blows.

"ACHOO!"
Funny sneezes.
Everyone goes flying!

They land in a place
with a nice view.

"Even the snow is soft
and furry," says Donald.

Donald, that is *not* snow!
That is a yeti!

This mountain is *not* a good place for a picnic.

Funny rolls past Mickey
and Minnie.

"ACHOO!"
Funny sneezes.
Everyone goes flying.

They land in a place with moonlight.

They are on the moon!

There might be something
wrong with Funny.

"I do not feel okay,"
says Funny.

"ACHOO!"
Funny sneezes.
Everyone lands in the snow.

"ACHOO!"
Funny sneezes.
Everyone lands in the desert.

"*ACHOO!*"
Funny sneezes.
Everyone lands at
the Funhouse.

Funny cannot stop
sneezing!

Funny sneezes only when
Minnie is close by.

It is the flower on
Minnie's hat!

Minnie puts the hat away.
Funny is all better!

It is time to start the picnic!
Funny chooses the place.

The Funhouse Forest is the best place for a picnic!